WHEN GUINEA PIGS FLY!

WHEN
GUINEA

James Proimos
& Andy Rheingold

ILLUSTRATIONS BY JAMES PROIMOS

Cartwheel
·B·O·O·K·S·®

An imprint of Scholastic Inc.

New York Toronto London Auckland Sydney
Mexico City New Delhi Hong Kong Buenos Aires

PIGS FLY!

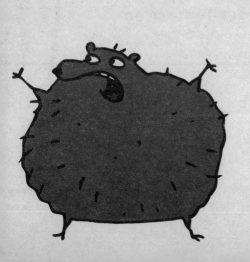

Library of Congress Cataloging-in-Publication Data Available

ISBN: 0-439-51902-0

10 9 8 7 6 5 4 3 2 1   05 06 07 08 09

Printed in the U.S.A.   40

First printing, June 2005

Book design by Alison Klapthor

For Amy
  —A.R.

For Jolie
  —J.P.

... PROLOGUE ...

I SPEND MOST MORNINGS, AND AFTERNOONS, AND NIGHTS, DREAMING ABOUT THE WORLD OUTSIDE *THE NATURAL PET.*

AURORA →

THE NATURAL PET IS NOT AN ORDINARY PET STORE. IT'S A SPECIAL PLACE, RUN BY A SPECIAL WOMAN NAMED AURORA.

AURORA HAS A UNIQUE WAY OF CARING FOR US. HER NEW AGE TREATMENTS KEEP US HAPPY AND HEALTHY WHILE WE WAIT FOR OUR NEW HOMES.

I'VE NEVER BEEN SO FIT!

OR SO STINKLESS!

I'M HAPPY AS A PIG IN SPECIALLY TREATED MUD!

IN FACT, EVERYBODY AT THE NATURAL PET IS SO HAPPY, NO ONE EVER WANTS TO LEAVE.

3

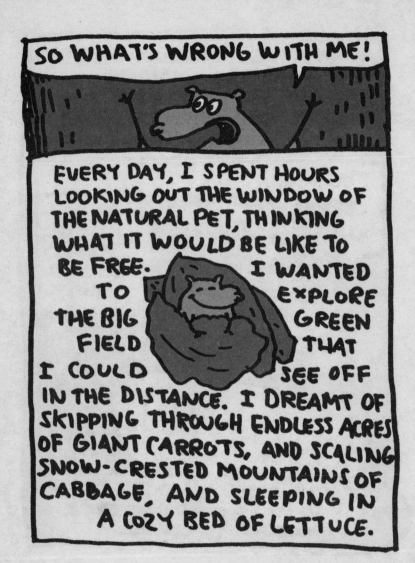

SO WHAT'S WRONG WITH ME!

EVERY DAY, I SPENT HOURS LOOKING OUT THE WINDOW OF THE NATURAL PET, THINKING WHAT IT WOULD BE LIKE TO BE FREE. I WANTED TO EXPLORE THE BIG GREEN FIELD THAT I COULD SEE OFF IN THE DISTANCE. I DREAMT OF SKIPPING THROUGH ENDLESS ACRES OF GIANT CARROTS, AND SCALING SNOW-CRESTED MOUNTAINS OF CABBAGE, AND SLEEPING IN A COZY BED OF LETTUCE.

Chapter One

I am deep, deep in thought, staring out the window, as usual, dreaming of the big, big green land outside. Suddenly, my daydream is interrupted.

"Hey, Brooks baby!" yells my cagemate Allen, a big, puffy guinea pig who likes to tell it like it is.

ALLEN

"Why do you waste your time daydreaming? Life outside is much more interesting. See?! Check out that giant pigeon. . . ."Allen points out.

"What pigeon?" I say. "I don't see any pigeon."

"The one that's flying right toward us!" Allen screams.

"Watch out!" I yell.

"I don't think he can hear you!" whispers my other cagemate and happy-go-lucky friend, Leone.

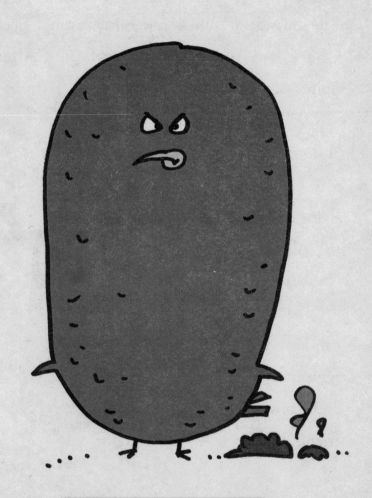

THE PIGEON

SPLAT!

The pigeon hits the glass.

"Do you think the pigeon wants to come in?" I ask.

"Maybe he needs glasses!" giggles Leone.

Allen ignores him.

"The point is, Brooksy boy, pigeons live on the Outside. And we live on the Inside. This is where we belong!"

"No one wants to leave this place," Leone adds.

"Am I right, gang?"

Chapter Two

The whole pet shop agrees.

"Yeah!" cries Leone. "I think we changed his mind. Thanks, everyone, for putting some sense into Brooks' head!"

Leone is so excited, he gives Allen a big hug.

Maybe everyone else feels that way, but not me. See, I want to be free. Suddenly, a thought pops into my mind that is quite strange, even for a guinea pig.

I am going to count to three and the next person who walks through The Natural Pet door will take me out of here.

Ready. Set. Go.

"One . . ." This is exciting. . . .

"Two . . ." Oh, boy!

"Three!" The doorknob turns!

This is it!

Freedom.

Chapter Three

Someone walks in the door, all right.

Oh, no! Not Needleman!

NEEDLE MAN

He comes in every single day. He never buys a pet. Not even a goldfish.

He walks over to Aurora. Needleman works over at Ye Olde Novelty Shoppe, which is a few doors down from The Natural Pet.

I think he likes Aurora.

Needleman just stands there. He stares at Aurora all googly-eyed, like an iguana.

Finally, Aurora speaks. "Well, what can I get you?" she asks.

"Um . . . well . . . um . . ." Needleman stammers, "I–I–I want to . . ."

NEEDLEMAN'S
TONGUE

"You want to . . . buy a pet?" she asks.

"Um, well, um . . ." Needleman is still tongue-tied.

"Scaly or furry?" Aurora asks.

"Yes!" shouts Needleman.

"Scaly?"

"Yes!"

"Or did you mean furry?"

"Yes!"

"I'm confused," says Aurora.

We all are.

"How about me?" I shout at the top of my chickpea-sized lungs.

"How about a guinea pig?" Aurora says.

She looks at Needleman with her big beautiful eyes, and Needleman smiles. "Yeah," he says, like he is in a trance. "I'll take them all."

I am so happy. My buddies, on the other hand, are going through a range of other emotions.

Aurora picks us out of our cage and puts us in a box.

Aurora is very sad and she starts to cry.

Chapter Four

Needleman pulls a handkerchief out of his pocket to help Aurora dry her tears. But it is a trick handkerchief from Ye Olde Novelty Shoppe— the kind you pull out of your pocket and you just keep pulling, and pulling, and pulling, and pulling. . . .

This only makes Aurora more hysterical.

In a panic, Needleman grabs the box with us guinea pigs and hightails it for the door.

Aurora starts waving the handkerchief and calling:

"Free! (sob) Set! (sob)

Free! (sob) Set! (sob)

Set! (sob) Free! (sob) . . ."

Needleman keeps on going. He doesn't look back. And neither do I.

In a flash, we are outside the pet shop.

Free at last.

I am all a-tingle.

The smell of the big-city air –

"Blueberries, I need blueberries!" cries Leone as we get thrown around in the box.

Needleman starts mumbling to himself. "What did she say when I was leaving? Something about free set? Or was it set free? Or . . ."

ME, ALL A-TINGLE

Aurora was trying to tell him that he gets a free set of healing gems with the purchase of any animal from The Natural Pet.

THE POSTER

Needleman keeps on walking and mumbling. "Hmmmm. Set free. Set free. Set free! That's it! She wants me to set these little piggies free! I know the perfect place—the park!"

"Did I hear that correctly? The park?! YIPPEE!" I scream.

Needleman starts running over to the big green guinea-pig paradise.

Needleman opens our box, dumps us out, and leaves us . . . alone.

I look around. And around.

And around. And around.

And around.

And around.

And around.

The big green place isn't exactly what I'd imagined.

Chapter Five

Chapter Six

There are no endless acres of carrots, no snow-crested mountains of cabbage, no cozy beds of lettuce.

Frankly, the whole big green place freaks me out. I am going to try to remain calm and act like all is cool. I look over at Leone and he is in a daze.

LEONE'S TINY MIN
WAS THINKING
WHAT IT WOULD
BE LIKE TO BE
A BLUEBERRY IN A
BOWL OF MILK.

"Well, boys," I say in a voice an octave deeper than usual, "we're all alone in the big, big, big, big world for the first time in our short, short, short, boring lives. Now is the time to gather up every ounce of courage, guts, strength, and pocket change."

But suddenly, a calm comes over me and I think to myself: Self, everything will be okay. Needleman is sure to see the "free set of gems" poster, and when he does, he will come back to get us.

We wait in the big green place for five minutes. That's like thirty minutes in guinea-pig time. Maybe more. It is enough time for us to pull ourselves together, and to become the guinea-pig superheroes we all know we are. And then I see the big black road.

How are we ever going to get across? Stay calm, I think.

That's when it occurs to me that I am a total nut for wishing to leave The Natural Pet. What was I thinking? We had it made back there. Free food. Clean water. State-of-the-art guinea-pig habitat. Bubble baths. It is scary out here. I want Aurora.

"You salad-head!" yells Allen. "Now that all your dreams have actually come true, what are we going to do?"

Leone's reaction is different. He starts singing and dancing.

"Oh, boy! Leone has finally gone off the deep end," Allen snarls at me. "He didn't have far to go, but this is all your fault, minnow-brain!"

"I'm not off the deep end! I'm on the high beginning!" Leone says.

"What?" Allen and I say at the same time.

"There's no place like home!" Leone points.

We follow the imaginary dash marks coming off of Leone's fingertip, and sure enough, we can see our beloved pet shop. And it isn't even all that far away!

But there is one problem. Would we make it across the street?

"C'mon, let's cross the street!" says Leone.

"Yep, when ya gotta go, ya gotta go!" says Allen.

"I'm not gonna step into the river of things that could squish me," I say.

WHAT ALLEN
WOULD LOOK LIKE
IF HE HAD BEEN
FLATTENED.

"Yes, you are," says Allen.

"No, I'm not!" I say.

"Yes, you are!"

"All right already, it's now or never!" I say. "And you can't stop me." I walk straight into the traffic without thinking. There are hundreds of feet and wheels all around me. But all I can see is a large lady in a polka-dot dress, and she's headed my way. She has on high heels, and they have my name on them.

Buh-bye.

Chapter Seven

So, here I am in the middle of the road– danger in front of me, danger behind me, danger on top of me. I am about to be squished by a pair of size-nine high heels, and my whole life is flashing before my eyes.

Suddenly, a set of tiny hands grabs me and pulls me out of harm's way. Well, it's two sets of tiny hands. Two of those hands belong to Leone. The other two, to Allen.

We quickly move back and forth and side to side, dodging everything. Imagine being

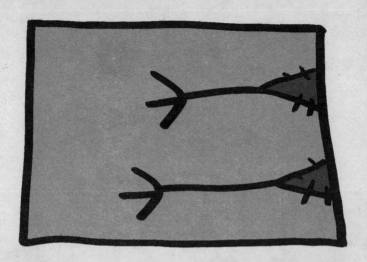

FOR A TOUGH GUY ALLEN HAD VERY SOFT HANDS.

in the middle of the biggest rainstorm you've ever seen and trying not to be hit by a raindrop. That's what it's like.

And that's when I notice it.

A giant wheel!

"That's it! Follow me, boys! To the giant wheel!" I shout.

"Brooks, ya nutjob! Are you stupid or just stupid? That giant wheel will flatten us like a pizza!"

In all the excitement, I think I hear Leone say, "I love pizza! Pizza and blueberries. Where do we make an order?"

I leap onto the giant wheel and start running around and around and around! Leone waves excitedly. "Look! It's like our exercise wheel back in the pet shop!"

Allen and Leone jump on board, and the three of us run and run and run inside the wheel until we are safely out of the road.

Suddenly, we see a gang of Rollerbladers! "That was close," we all say together.

The only danger now is the three of us falling down from laughing so hard from the fun we just had.

But Leone, Allen, and I are no closer to finding our way home to The Natural Pet. We're completely lost.

Meanwhile.....

NEEDLEMAN TRYS OUT HIS "FINDING THE PIGGIES" MAGNIFYING GLASS.

Chapter Eight

We walk around in a daze. Everything is so big and tall. There are trees, and behind the trees, tall skyscrapers. And we are very, very small.

"You don't look like you're from around here," says a voice that is not Leone's or Allen's or mine. A squirrel leaps from the top of one of the trees and lands right in front of us.

"What gave us away?" I ask.

"You are looking up. Tourists always look up," the squirrel explains.

"Oh, really? Is that it?" I respond.

"And the giant camera around your neck," adds the squirrel. I look down, and the squirrel laughs. "Gotcha!"

Allen and Leone laugh, too.

The squirrel introduces herself. Her name is Rosie. We explain we are looking for a way home, if only we knew where home was. Rosie offers to give us a tour of the park.

"But before we go anywhere–remember this–you better watch out for the giant pigeons. They eat everything, and I mean

EVERYTHING,"

Rosie warns us.

GIANT
PIGEON
TEETH

Rosie puts two of her fingers to her giant squirrel buckteeth and whistles loudly. Two of her squirrel buddies appear from the trees.

"Hop on!" Rosie shouts. And that's what we do. Each of us jumps on the back of a squirrel. And the squirrels run all over the park and give us a whirlwind tour.

THEY TOOK US EVERY WHERE!

THE CASTLE!

THE
BOAT
POND!

EVEN THE ZOO!

Chapter Nine

What a tour! Even Allen, who hates most everything, seems to enjoy it. We wave good-bye to Rosie and her pals.

"Now what?" Allen asks. "We still have no stinkin' clue how to get home."

"I hear music and party and fun! Don't you hear it, too?" says Leone.

Shhh. I think I hear something. . . .

Shhh . . .

Yes.

Leone is right.

That does sound like a party in the distance.

We follow the noise.

And this is our first big mistake.

Rosie had warned us about the pigeons, but she didn't say anything about the . . . rats. Big, ugly, smelly, ugly, big rats.

The biggest of the big, ugly, smelly, ugly, big rats speaks up.

"We hate every non-rat animal in the world. Do you know what we do to non-rat-style individuals when we find them?"

THE BIGGEST OF THE BIG UGLY SMELLY UGLY BIG RATS

"Give them a hug and send them on their way?" Leone says hopefully.

The big rat looks around at his fellow rats.

"AHEM. WHAT WE DO TO THEM iS SOOOOOOOO GRUESOME . . ."

"How gruesome is it?" the rats call back.

"So gruesome that it is more gruesome than snake food," he says.

The other rats laugh like evil villains laugh.

The big rat waves his hand and everyone stops laughing. Except Leone.

Allen and I are not laughing, of course. We're too busy shaking.

The big rat grabs me. He looks right into my eyes.

Leone finally stops laughing. He either realizes we are in serious trouble, or he is catching his breath before laughing some more.

The big rat then says, "But we love other rats! And I see by your eyes that you guys are rats!"

Leone starts to say, "Rats? Wrong! We're guinea pigs!" But luckily for us, I shove my tiny hand all the way into Leone's mouth so no one hears him.

The big rat shouts, "Welcome to our 'invitation only' rat party, fellow rats!"

He gives me a big hug. Then he hugs Allen. Then Leone.

Then Leone hugs every rat.

"Let's paaaar-rrrrrrty!"

shouts the big rat.

HIS MOUTH SAID "LET'S PARTY" BUT HIS BREATH SAID "RUN!"

Chapter Ten

Party Photos

Me

Allen & Some rat

Leone in a Lampshade.

Leone took this
picture of his feet.

We played pin the
tail on me.

What's with Allen?

Chapter Eleven

What a party! Oh, boy!

Well, until Allen suddenly loses it. He can't play the rat anymore. He is the kind of guy who has to tell it like it is. You have to admire a guy like that.

"WE'RE NOT RATS, YOU STUPID MUSH-HEADED RODENTS!" he screams.

I'm pretty sure we are all dead meat.

HERE LIES
BROOKS.
HE WAS QUITE
HEALTHY UNTIL
ALLEN OPENED
HIS BIG MOUTH.

"YOU GUYS ARE ABOUT TO BECOME DEAD MEAT!" yells the big rat.

Dozens of rats surround us in all their big, ugly, smelly grossness.

"Any last words?" says the big rat as his brothers grab us.

"Blueberry!" shouts out Leone. "That's a good last word!"

I have to do something quick. I hold up my paw and launch into the greatest speech of my life.

"My friends. Aren't we all the same underneath our big, smelly exteriors? Do you not cry when it's bedtime? Of course you do. And so do we. So please, if you have a heart at all, go and help all the creatures in the world, for we are all brothers, even the girls."

And I swear, the rats do like I say.

They leave.

Pronto.

Without even saying good-bye.

"I'm gonna miss them rats," says Leone, wiping a tear from his eye.

"They were about to rip us apart, you knuckle-belly!" Allen reminds him.

"Still, Brooks made a nice speech," Leone notes.

"My speech had nothing to do with the rats leaving," I say with a gulp, as I point upward.

A flock of giant pigeons is circling above us. "That's what chased away the rats."

"But you did make a fine speech!" says Leone.

Allen has to answer: "No, he didn't!"

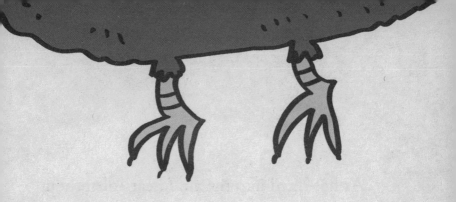

I interrupt my friends. "You two might want to continue this discussion later."

A particularly mean-looking pigeon is heading down toward us at an incredible rate of speed!

Leone takes off to the left.

I take off to the right.

Allen takes off straight up.

Yep. That's right. The pigeon got Allen.

As he's lifted into the air, I hear Allen shout at Leone, "Brooks made a lousy speech, dirt-sack!"

Another pigeon has me in her sights.

I run

    and

        run

           and

              run

                until

                  I can't

                    run

                      anymore.

Then I hide inside a plastic cup where no one can see me.

When I look up, the sky is pigeonless. I am safe. But where is Leone? And what is going to happen to Allen? You can imagine how much I would like to hear Allen call me a "dirt-sack." I think I'll cry until I fall asleep.

NEEDLEMAN THOUGHT IF HE DRESSED LIKE ONE OF THE GUINEA PIGS THEY WOULD BE EASIER TO FIND.

Chapter Twelve

Now that Brooks is asleep, let me tell some of the story. Hey, it's me, Leone.

Well, I'm all by myself.

This is loads of fun.

But now it's a little less fun.

Now I'm having a little more fun.

Now a little less.

Now more.

Now I'm having no fun at all.

I miss my friends.

Turn the page, I'm gonna cry.

Too late.

Chapter Thirteen

It's me, Brooks.

I'm all alone, crying myself to sleep. It's the middle of the night and I hear the most horrible sound. It's a growl that turns into a deep roar, followed by a high-pitched screech like nails on a chalkboard.

My imagination is running wild with what the strange noise might be.

WAS IT A BEAR EATING A PICNIC BASKET?

AND A WOMAN
SCREAMING?

WHILE A WASHING MACHINE
SLIDES DOWN A HILL?

The noise is coming from right over the hill behind me. I keep imagining more and more crazy things causing this sound. But my fear is taken over by curiosity.

I creep up over the hill.

"YOU'VE GOT TO BE KIDDING!" I scream without thinking.

And I wake up a tiny, tiny cockroach.

The cockroach screams back, "Hey, why you wanna go and wake up Da Mayor!"

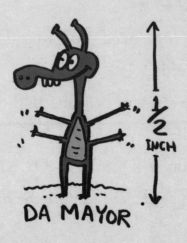

½ INCH

DA MAYOR

"I'm sorry, but you were so loud!" I say.

"It's just that I'm allergic to all this grass," the cockroach explains.

I don't understand a word the cockroach just said except the first part. "Did you say you were the mayor?" I ask.

"Nope, not me, I didn't say that."

"I thought you did."

"I said I was Da Mayor, and I is."

"My two friends are missing. I must find them ASAP."

"Hey, no need to s-p-e-l-l your big college words."

"Well, can you help me find them as soon as possible?"

"Of course I can. I'm Da Mayor. Would you be so kind as to tell me the names of your lost friends?"

"Leone," I say. And before I can add, "And Allen," Da Mayor is off screaming.

"LEOOONNNNNEEEE!"

"All you're doing is yelling his name!" I say.

"Do you know a better way to find someone who is lost?"

I don't. I join in.

Chapter Fourteen

"LEOONNNNNNE!"

Then we hear a third voice yelling "Leone."

We get closer to it.

And closer.

And closer.

Until that voice and the body that is screaming is right in front of us.

And guess who it is?

It's Leone himself!

"Why are you screaming your own name?" I ask.

"I just want to help!" Leone answers.

I'm so happy to see Leone that this makes sense to me.

"Now we have to find my other best buddy, Allen. The giant pigeons have him!" I say to Da Mayor.

"The pigeons! Why didn't you say so?!" said Da Mayor. Then he whistles and another half-inch-sized cockroach comes running over. "Get on our backs. We'll locate them!"

"You're joking, right?" I ask.

"GET ON OUR BACKS! NOOOOWWW!!!!!"

screams Da Mayor's little friend.

And we do just that.

Chapter Fifteen

YOU FOUND ME!
IT'S OUR FRIEND!
WOW. I THOUGHT HE WAS JUST ANOTHER BUMP IN THE ROAD.

Chapter Sixteen

So we find Allen. And there is joy in all of our hearts. We were apart for a whole night. That's like a whole week in guinea-pig time.

"How did you get away from the pigeons?" I ask Allen.

Allen acts out everything that happened with him and the pigeons. Unfortunately, we are all standing a tad too close to him as he tells his story.

But we don't care. Allen, Leone, and I are reunited! Back together again! And still far from home!

We are so excited.

Suddenly, a little boy steps in front of us. An evil, terrible, nasty little boy.

He picks up Allen, Leone, and myself with his stubby little hands. Da Mayor and his buddy grab onto his ankles and they start gnawing on them in an attempt to free us.

But it gets worse. The boy takes out his gum and sticks it on the back of Leone's head. Then the little brat ties us to his water rocket.

He counts down.

10
9
8
7
6
5
4
3
2
1!

Blast

off!

The boy launches us into the air.

Going up is nice.

Going down is not.

We are hurtling toward our deaths.

But then at the last second, we start going back up!

I scream with joy . . .

. . . until I see that it is a pigeon that is carrying us upward!

I scream.

Leone screams.

Allen says, "Hey, Walter, how's it going?"

"It's goin' really peachy, Allen baby," the pigeon answers. "We miss you big-time!"

"Huh?" I ask.

"Huh?" Leone says.

"Uh-huh," says Allen.

That's right. Allen is a friend of the pigeon!

Chapter Seventeen

Walter fills us in on what really happened with Allen and the pigeons.

WE TOOK ALLEN TO OUR CASTLE. WE NEEDED A FOURTH HAND FOR OUR CARD GAME.

HE STARTED CRYING LIKE A BIG BABY. "DON'T EAT ME!"

BUT SOON ALL HE COULD TALK ABOUT WAS HOW MUCH HE MISSED YOU GUYS.

SO I FLEW HIM BACK TO THE SPOT WHERE I FIRST FOUND HIM.

AND THAT WAS THAT.

. . . .

Chapter Eighteen

From way up here, everything looks so small. I quickly scan below for The Natural Pet.

"Hey! There's that Needleman guy sitting on a park bench!" yells Leone.

"That goof-wad can get us back home!" adds Allen.

"We'll gather enough force to crash through Chapter Nineteen and into Needleman's lap if Walter drops us right. . . ."

Chapter Nineteen

And

we fall

and

fall

and

fall

and

fall

and

fall

and

fall

and

fall.

Chapter Twenty

Plunk! We land right in Needleman's lap.

"I found them! I found them!" cheers Needleman.

"He found us! He found us!" cheer we.

Needleman runs down into the subway with us and gets on the first train that shows up.

There we sit, four of the happiest guys in the world.

There's nothing like going home.

Chapter Twenty-one

Needleman is so excited that when we get to our stop he runs off the train faster than I have ever seen a human run. He is probably thinking about all the different reactions Aurora will have when he tells her he found the guinea pigs.

As the subway door closes, we can see Needleman looking back.

Only Needleman forgets one thing.

Us!

On the train!

To be continued . . .

About the authors

James Proimos has garnered critical acclaim for previous children's books including *Cowboy Boy*, *The Loudness of Sam*, and the *Johnny Mutton* series. He lives in Venice, CA, and on a farm in Maryland with his wife and kids.

Andy Rheingold has written numerous cartoons for Nickelodeon Animation, MTV, and the Cartoon Network. He lives in New York City with his wife and two sons.